KT-497-657

Fingers in the yogurts

written by Marie Birkinshaw
illustrated by Serena Feneziani

Dad had been shopping.

We all helped to put
the things away.

Tom put the bananas
in the fruit basket.

6

Sally put the cheese
in the fridge.

Dad put the chocolate
on the top shelf.

Sarah put her fingers
in the yogurts and...

we were **all** put outside!

Under the sky

written by Lorraine Horsley
illustrated by Amanda Wood

Under the sky is the sun.

Under the sun is a tree.

Under the tree is a branch.

Under the branch is me.

Under me is a rock.

Under the rock is the ground.

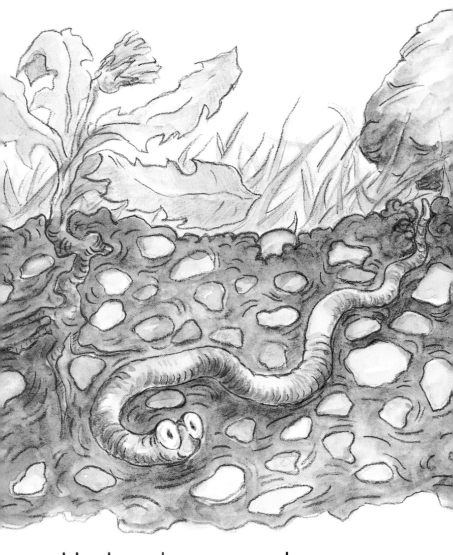

Under the ground
   is a big pink worm...
Wriggling and squiggling
   around.

Nina's new puppy

written by Marie Birkinshaw
illustrated by Julie Anderson

Nina and her family had
a new puppy.

First the puppy chewed
Dad's boots.
Nina laughed.

Then the puppy chewed
Mum's gloves. Nina
laughed again.

But when the puppy chewed
Nina's books, Nina didn't
laugh. Nina was cross.

And when the puppy
chewed Nina's **rabbit**,

Bad dog!

Nina was so cross that she went back to the shop...

Now Nina's puppy has something of his **own** to chew.

Beaker Squeaker

written by Shirley Jackson
illustrated by David Mostyn

Beaker Squeaker
sat on a wall.

Beaker Squeaker
had a red ball.

Beaker Squeaker
ran over the chairs.

Beaker Squeaker
ran down the stairs.

Beaker Squeaker
ran over the floor.

Beaker Squeaker
ran round the door.

Beaker Squeaker
went out through her flap.

Beaker Squeaker
went for a nap.

Beaker Squeaker

Read the first line of this rhyme to your child and encourage her to read the rest to you, with your help. Can she point to the words that rhyme? See if you can read it together a little quicker each time.

Does Beaker Squeaker remind you of a nursery rhyme?

New words

Encourage your child to use some of these new words to help her to write her own very simple stories and rhymes.

One or two sentences is great. Go back to look at earlier books and their wordlists to practise other words.

is specially designed to help your child learn to read. It will complement all the methods used in schools.

Parents took part in extensive research to ensure that **Read with Ladybird** would help your child to:

- take the first steps in reading
- improve early reading progress
- gain confidence in new-found abilities.

The research highlighted that the most important qualities in helping children to read were that:

- books should be fun – children have enough 'hard work' at school
- books should be colourful and exciting
- stories should be up to date and about everyday experiences
- repetition and rhyme are especially important in boosting a child's reading ability.

The stories and rhymes introduce the 100 words most frequently used in reading and writing.

These 100 key words actually make up half the words we use in speech and reading.

The three levels of **Read with Ladybird** consist of 22 books, taking your child from two words per page to 600-word stories.

Read with Ladybird will help your child to master the basic reading skills so vital in everyday life.

Ladybird have successfully published reading schemes and programmes for the last 50 years. Using this experience and the latest research, **Read with Ladybird** has been produced to give all children the head start they deserve.